Out in the sticks, a long way from the city,
A small village sits, filled with flowers, so pretty.

Each cottage is thatched with a ton of straw,
You simply can't help but feel in awe.

On Wander Road lives an old man and his wife,
A lady who gives him the happiest life.

From dancing,
  dreaming and doing
    wonderful things,

She makes him feel richer than all of the kings.

Their garden looks like a fairytale,
Onlookers send them so much mail.
'What beautiful flowers that peek over your fence,'
Why they were tall made absolutely no sense.

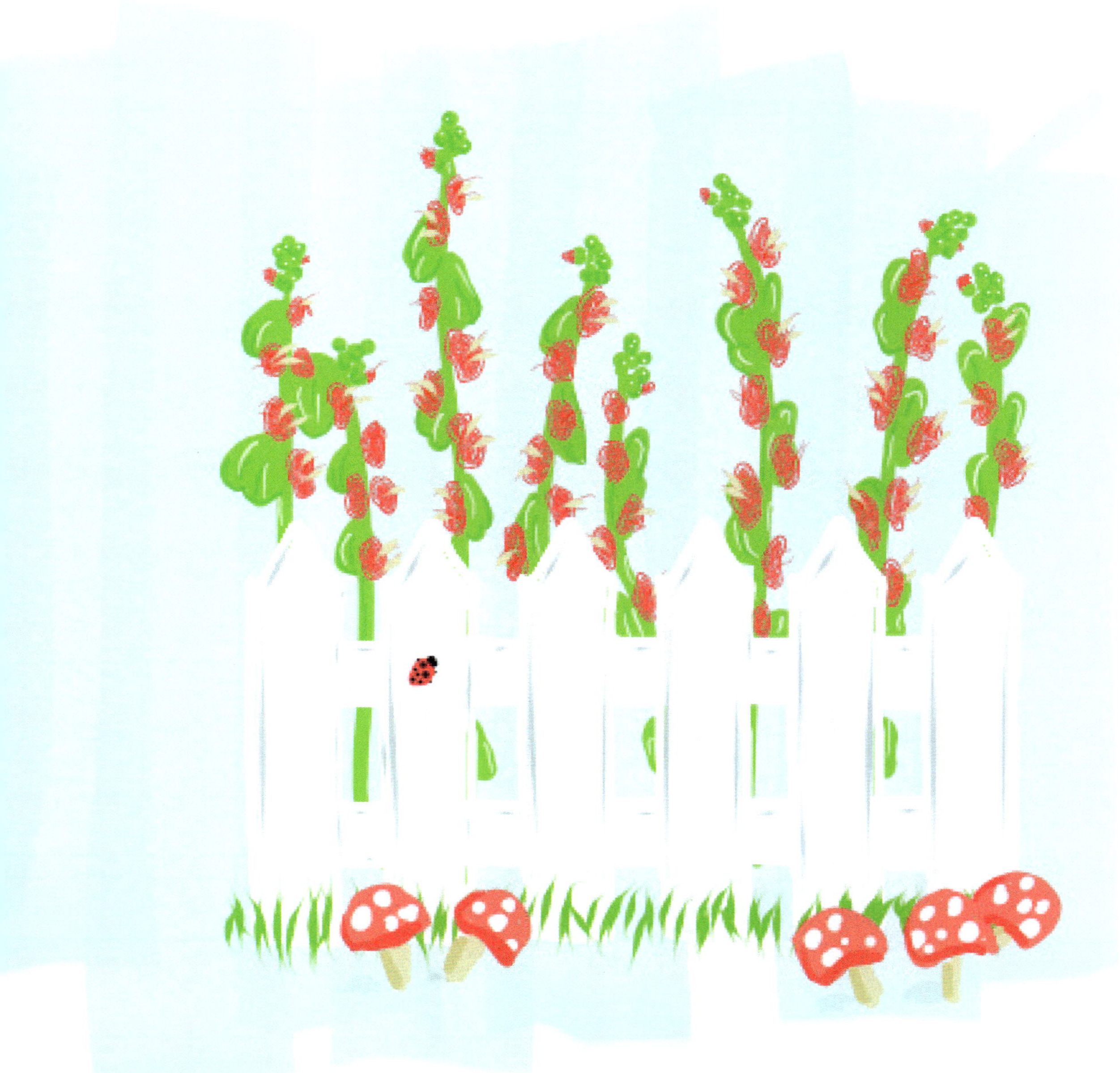

The youngest of plants; Daisy, Tulip and Rose,

They loved to play with the garden hose.

So much in fact, they abused their power
and often gave Callum an unwanted shower.

Callum was the only one,
Who really was loved by none.
For weeks he stood with big, blue eyes,
While the three of them told him lies.

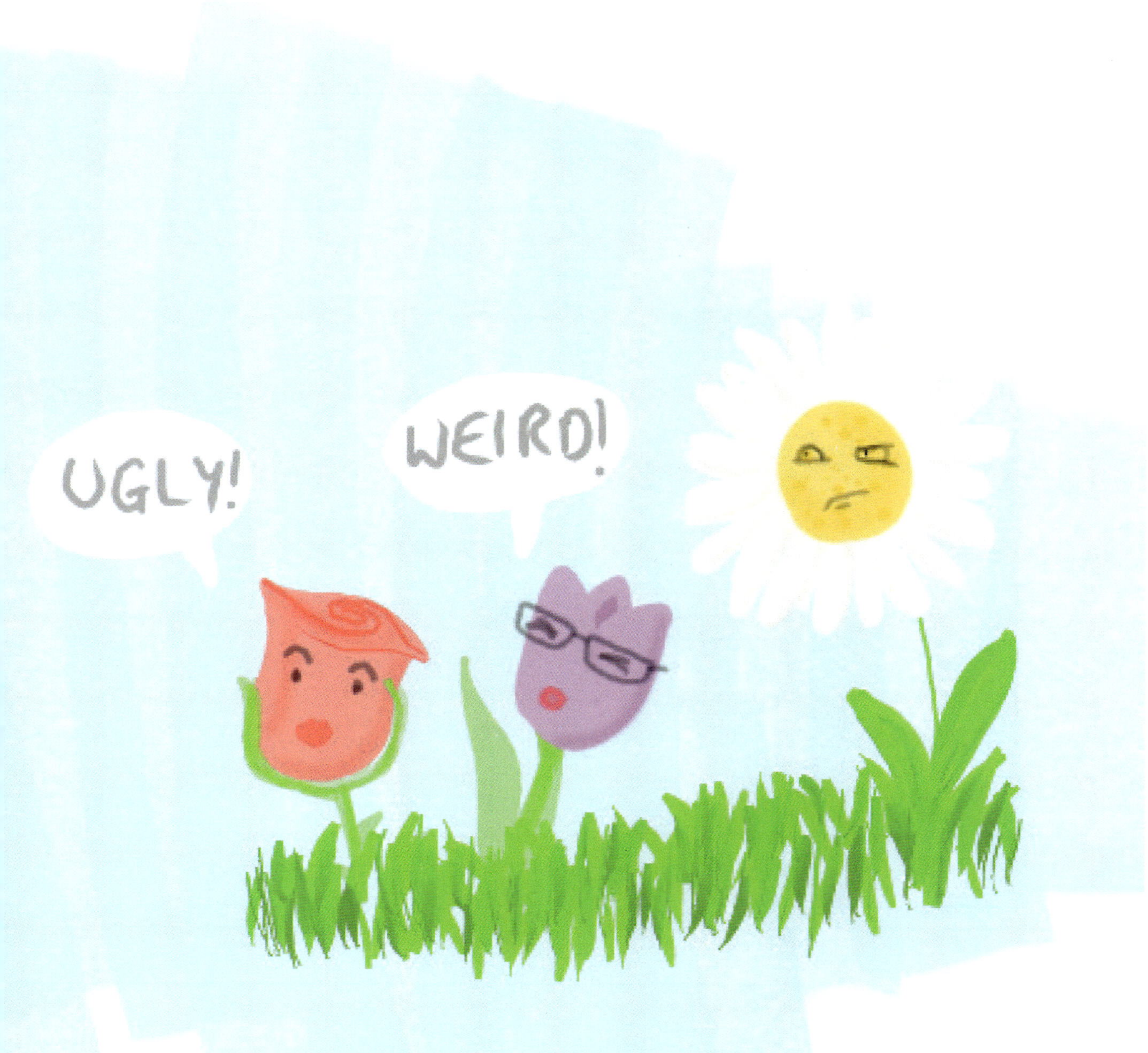
UGLY!
WEIRD!

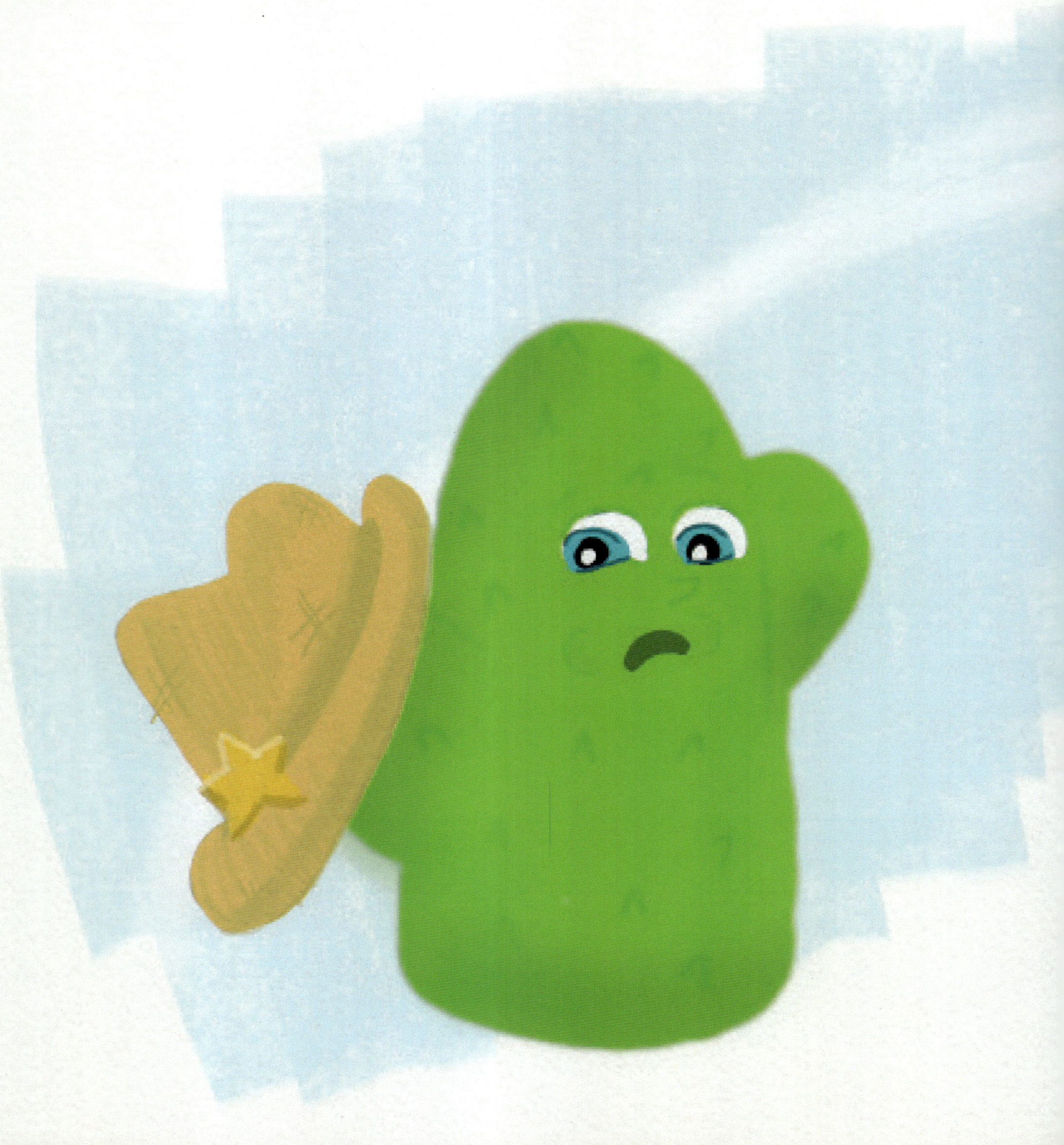

They even found an
old tatty hat,
And tossed it at him,
how naughty is that?
He could not help his prickly skin,
They made him feel like he belonged in the bin.

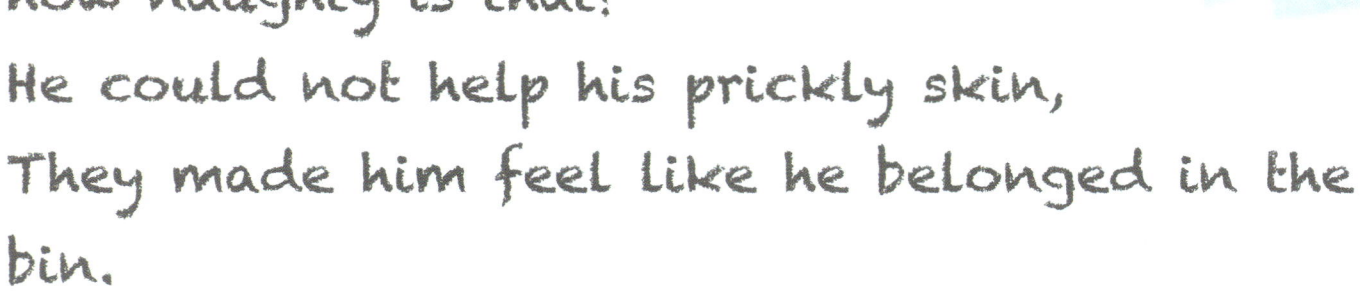

They teased him rotten and made fun,
So much so, Callum yearned to run.

He was so sad, longing for a friend,
For maybe then his heart would mend.

All of a sudden from the sky,
Something descended towards
Callum's eye.

Big and red, as red as cherry,
   A beaming smile, big and merry.

It tangled itself around Callum's prickles, He could not help but laugh and said 'It really tickles!'

'Hi my name's Henry, I'm sorry, I'm stuck', Callum replied 'No, it's fine. I'm nice, you're in luck.

The two were chatting and laughing away,
At the situation they had themselves in today.

HA HA

For how could it be?
What are the chances?
Callum's happiness
immediately enhances.

As weeks pass by and the sun grows hotter, the flowers desperately needed some water.

They looked at Callum with despise,
For from Callum they heard no cries.

They wondered why he was not thirsty,
Which was when Henry shouted
'He's a cactus isn't he?'

They replied
'He's a monster, how can he be fine?
For he must be thirsty, yet he does not whine.'

Henry explained how special cacti are,
For a little water can go far.

They store their drink inside their stem,
And one drink a year is enough for them.

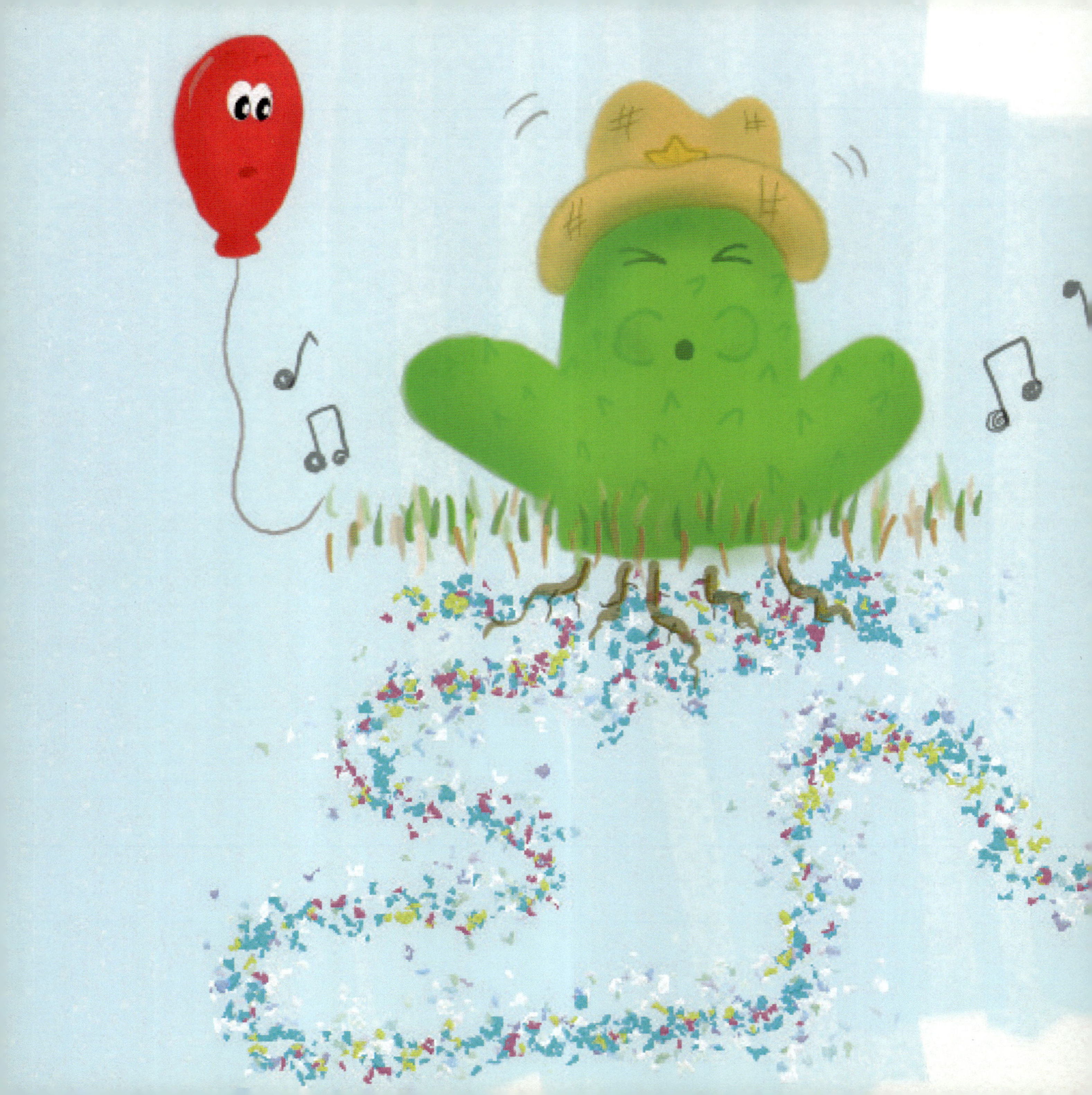

Suddenly Callum beams 'I have an idea!'
He squeezed really tight while the flowers sneer.

He pumps some water under the ground,
Followed by a magical sound.

One by one the flowers yelled 'Hip, Hip Hooray!'

"HOORAY"

It really took their breath away.

For Callum who they taunted and teased,
Had shared his water, they were so pleased.

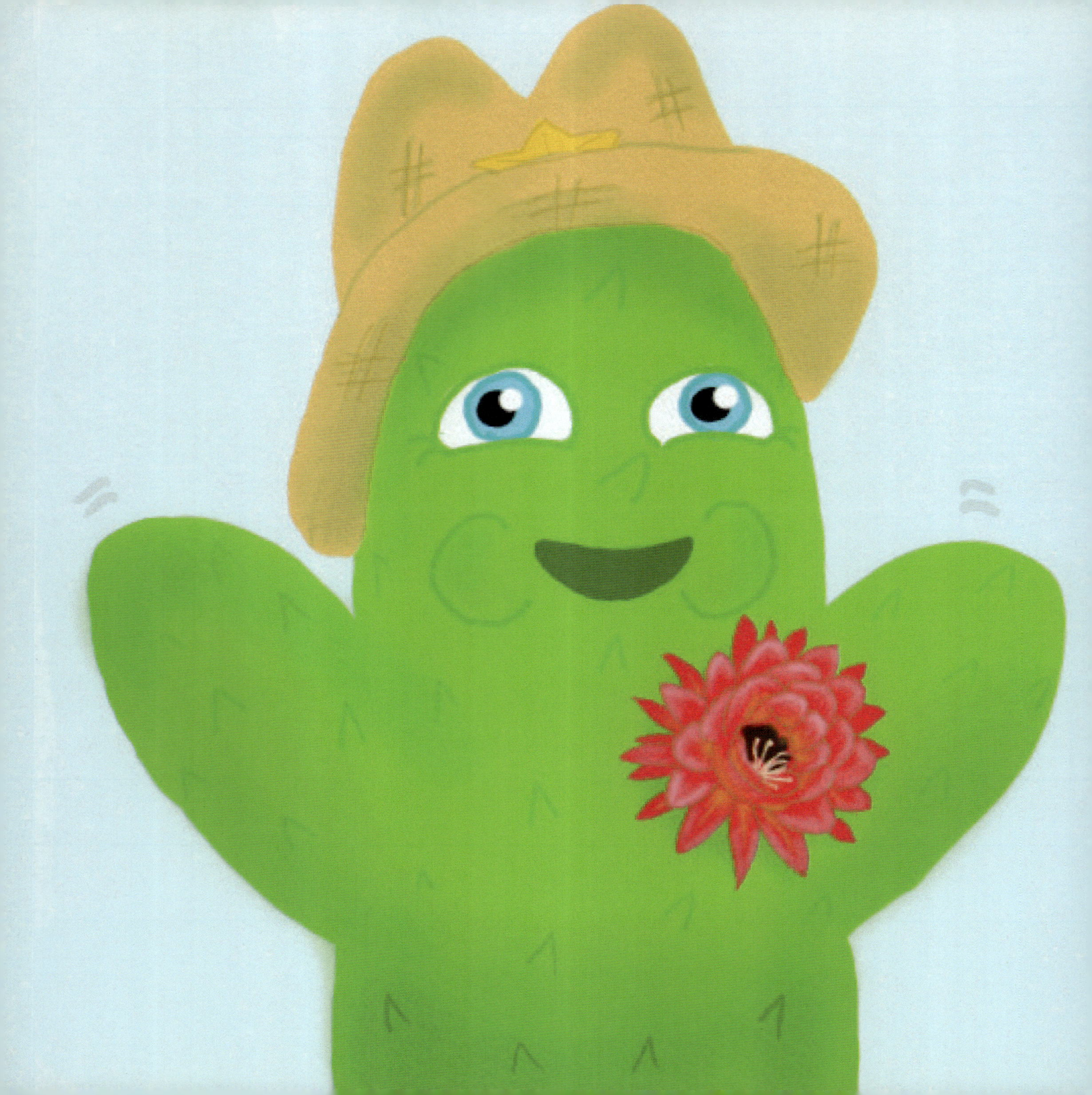

Callum and the flowers became the
best of friends,
The love for one another, it never ends.

Callum's happiness could not be doubted,
And from his chest, a big, bright flower
sprouted.

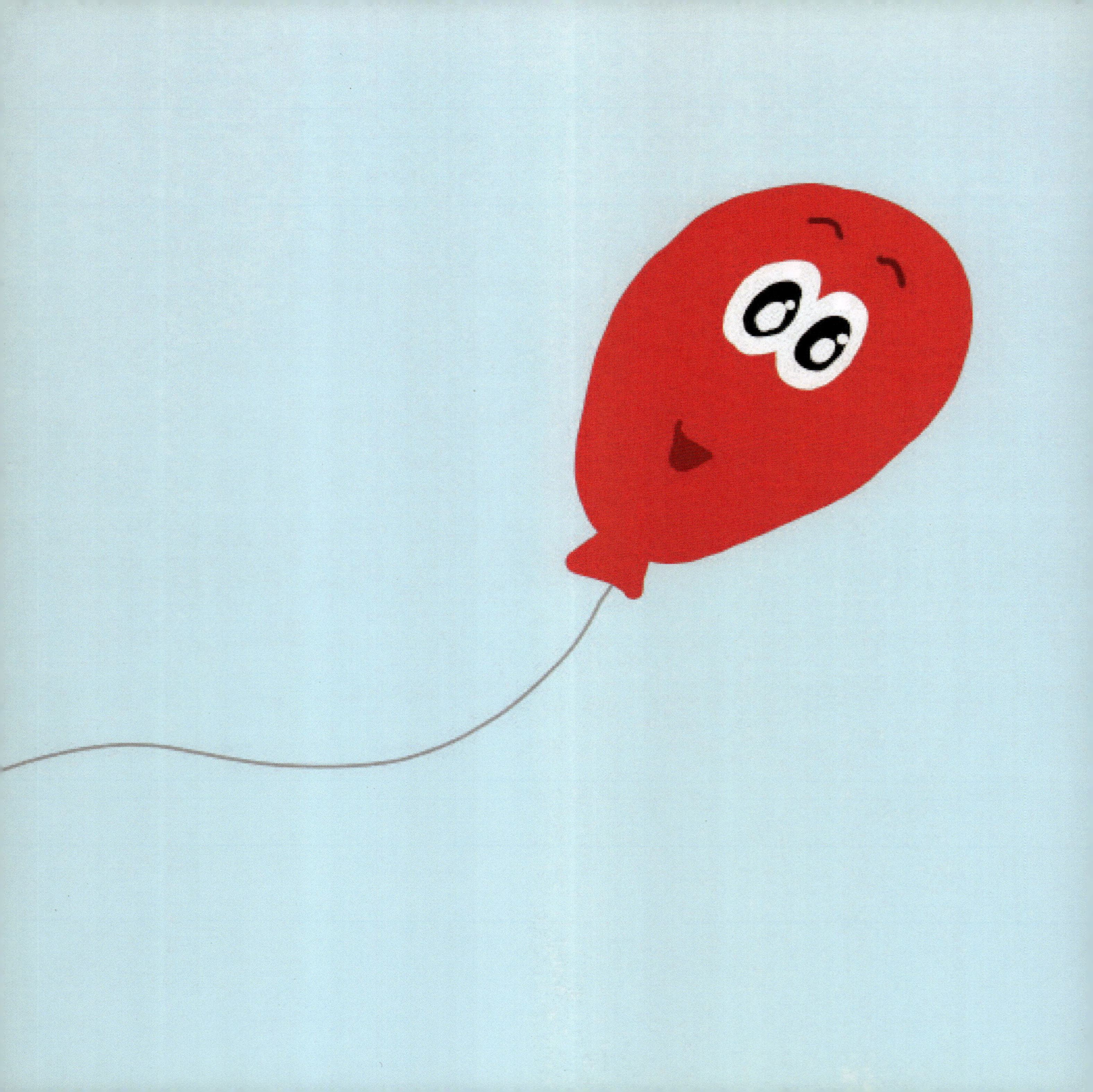

Printed in Great Britain
by Amazon